MW01503669

FIVE FACES
OF
FELICIA
CLARKE

Also by Alexandria Blaelock

FIVE FACES
OF
FELICA
CLARKE

ALEXANDRIA BLAELOCK

Bluemere Books
MELBOURNE, AUSTRALIA

Ordering Information:
Discounts are available on quantity purchases. For details, contact orders@bluemerebooks.com.

Five Faces of Felicia Clarke/Alexandria Blaelock
hardback ISBN: 978-1-922744-16-6
paperback ISBN: 978-1-922744-17-3
digital ISBN: 978-1-922744-18-0

Book Layout © BookDesignTemplates.com

BlueMere Books
www.bluemerebooks.com

Contents

INTRODUCTION

Here in Australia, we don't have a Thanksgiving day *per se*.

Except for Norfolk Island, where half the population are descended from the *Bounty* Mutineers[1]. And goodness knows they've a lot to be thankful for.

The islanders celebrate their arrival on Anniversary Day (June 8th), sixty-six years after the mutineers first burned the *Bounty* at Pitcairn Island.

Norfolk Island was settled by the British shortly after the 1788 arrival of the First Fleet as a commercial development come penal colony.

But by 1855 they'd abandoned it in favour of imprisoning people at home. It became an Australian territory in 1914.

But I digress.

Thanksgiving.

---

[1] This is, of course, a gross exaggeration for the sake of a good story. The actual figure is more like a third.

I generally do it around New Years.

As I half-heartedly do my Hogmanay cleaning.

And if you've read my blog at all you'll know how much I detest cleaning. Especially now my new dog (Clever Girl), the black double-coated lab has come to stay with us.

I was the one who wrote *Ms Blaelock's Book of Minimally Viable Housekeeping* after all.

Though in my defence, it *is* Summer here, and there are way better things to do.

So minimally viable housekeeping done, we have a barbecue and sit on the deck with a few beers.

Sweating gently in the heat.

There's a sacrificial sausage up the other end for the hornets and magpies to fight over, and a citronella candle under the table repelling the legions of mosquitoes.

And we talk about those who've left us; the good and the bad, some taken too soon and some too late, the ones we miss and the ones we don't.

As the Rabbie Burns poem goes:

> "Should Old Acquaintance be forgot,
> and never thought upon;
> The flames of Love extinguished,
> and fully past and gone:
> Is thy sweet Heart now grown so cold,

that loving Breast of thine;

That thou canst never once reflect

On old long syne."

Over time, one of my bookshelves has become a memorial.

Photos of all my past dogs, cats, friends and relatives are lined up where I can see them.

And here and there amongst them, their significant gifts; an angel clock, an old teddy bear, a beer stein, and many more.

Some of these artefacts have appeared in my other stories.

Among the artefacts are photos of those we've lost in other ways; through divorce, the passage of time or never having the chance to become close friends.

They're all right there, exactly where I can look up from my computer to see them.

So maybe it's more the beers than my memories that make me maudlin as I reminisce. Though I suspect that's part of my cultural heritage too.

Or course, we never really know other people, only the faces they choose to show us.

The stories in this collection are about Felicia Clarke, but they're based, in some way, on the people enshrined in my bookshelf.

- For Love of Felicia - Tom goes to secretarial college, falls in love, and... well... doesn't get married.
- The Secretarial Shelter - Charles hires a new secretary and sees his business grow.
- My Lucky Customer - Erol opens a shop, and believes his first customer brings him luck.
- Stranger Danger - a girl meets a stranger who encourages her to follow her dreams.
- Best Friends Forever - Etta takes a trip down memory lane when she runs into the woman who was once her best friend.

So I hope you enjoy this collection, and make some time over the next few weeks to keep the memories of those you've lost alive.

Alexandria Blaelock
Melbourne, Australia
December, 2021

FOR LOVE OF FELICIA

Tom died relatively young.

Some would say too young; that he never really lived.

But by the end of his life, the way Tom looked at it, he'd met the love of all of his lives, and they'd done about as much as was possible, and he was satisfied with that.

Couldn't have asked for more.

Except that she'd married him of course, but other than that, nothing more.

Felicia was his first and only love, and he met her through a series of extraordinary circumstances at secretarial college.

He'd been working in a dead-end haulage job when his new employer took a chance on him, and his mathematical abilities.

Tom was so very grateful to leave his days of hefting boxes and bags on his back as he dodged nuggets of fresh horse shit and steaming rivulets of piss on the cobblestones.

So grateful he'd signed up to the college the very next day, vowing to make the best of it.

He did not miss the days when in his worn-out, newspaper padded boots missed their mark and landed squarely in the mess.

Nor did he miss the dust and ground-up manure getting in his eyes and ears, and smeared across his face and neck as he mopped up his dripping sweat with his filthy handkerchief.

Or staggering into a storeroom and trying to stack the goods more or less neatly before he collapsed underneath their weight.

Not in the slightest.

But he loved his new job, safe and sound and warm in the office. Even if he did have to stand all day at his desk, trying not to blot the account books with his leaky fountain pen.

The first chance he got; he was buying a new one. The best he could afford. Perhaps even something inlaid with celluloid.

And every day since, he thanked his dead parents for interceding. For getting him out of that mess and into a new, more respectable life and place of employment.

And into college where he met the one and only Felicia who changed the course of his life.

Felicia seemed like one of those ancient Greek goddesses; helpful, and very capable in an exotically no-nonsensically efficient way.

When she smiled her lopsided smile at him, revealing her one true flaw, he was a goner.

Fell good and hard, no holds barred, no returns in love with her.

Loved the way she tilted her head.

Loved the way a single tendril of brown hair broke free from her bun and curled lovingly around her neck.

Loved the bafflingly enigmatically crooked little finger of her left hand.

Fortunately, the class tutor arbitrarily grouped the class into pairs, and he was paired with her.

For ten whole weeks of evening classes.

And that meant, ten weeks of study groups and research trips outside of class hours.

It was a godsend.

At the time, he'd just moved out of the boarding house and was living alone in a tiny apartment in the city, quite near the college.

Naturally, she lived at home with her parents in the suburbs; a train ride away followed by a brisk twenty-minute walk.

However, they both worked in the City.

He made quick work of suggesting they met at the close of business in a small café near the college for a bite to eat before class.

Ostensibly to discuss their progress on their one assessable assignment.

But in reality, to charm her.

And conveniently, it seemed she didn't take much charming.

Not that she was anyone's, as evidenced by her swift and brutal rebuff of John Stone's advances.

But she was certainly amenable to his.

And he loved her even more for that.

That she dressed and acted modestly.

That she smelled of Ivory soap.

And her hand, when he first dared to touch it, was as soft as butter.

Not the rock hard in winter kind of butter, but the summer soft in the larder kind of butter.

After a while, she started to call at his apartment to collect him for their field trips.

The first time she arranged to call by, he walked home a foot above the ground.

But when he got home, and looked around his apartment, he promptly fell back to earth with a thump.

Panicked at the filthy, musty old place.

So he rolled up his sleeves and cleaned the place. Thoroughly with scalding hot water, carbolic soap, and elbow grease.

Then bought a table and a couple of chairs, a curtain to hang at the window, and a couple of new cups and saucers on the never-never so she didn't run screaming from the place.

And on the morning of the day she was due, a small bunch of fresh, cheerful daffodils to welcome her.

Then back out on the street to scavenge a plain, barely chipped pickle jar from the local trash to sit them in.

Felicia professed to be charmed by his digs and assured him she found them as neat, and clean as she had imagined.

Tom surreptitiously wiped his brow.

And made himself a promise that he would clean his apartment once a week, and tidy up every day before he left for work, just in case she called unexpectedly in the future.

Which of course she did.

The very next day as a matter of fact.

And every single one after that.

Blushing prettily, claiming to maybe have left something or other behind the previous day.

Tom wasn't fooled.

Though he was a little excited at her forwardness.

The first time he kissed her, was when he walked her to the train station after class.

On the bridge over the train line, in the days before you could enter from both sides.

The lamplight reflected from the low hanging clouds and glistened on the tracks as he leaned forward to pull her coat more closely around her neck to be sure she didn't catch a cold.

Suddenly, somehow, they were kissing.

Tom had no real idea what he was doing, but it seemed Felicia was in no way uncertain, as she wound her arms around his neck and pulled him closer to her.

He impudently put his arms beneath her open overcoat, linking them behind her back.

The kiss was magnificent.

He never wanted it to end.

But she had a train to catch - the last train of the day in fact, and he reluctantly let her go.

Though it wasn't much longer before he kind of, sort of, delayed her return so long she missed the train.

Not that she was upset about that.

Or even that she was forced to stay over at his place for the lack of having enough money to stay anywhere else.

Knowing she couldn't contact her parents and tell them not to worry.

He started to feel guilty.

But later that night, in his moonlit bedroom, as he peeled the clothes, one by one from her willing body, the feeling eased.

And as he revelled in her soft, creamy skin, the faded smell of lavender stuffed drawer sachets, and the warmth of her body, he forgot it altogether.

She must have suffered some kind of repercussion for her overnight absence, but she never breathed a word of it to him.

Just made sure that they didn't waste any time dawdling between class and his apartment, and making sure she made it to the station with plenty of time to spare for the last train.

And of course, as time passed, he asked her to marry him.

She was reluctant, as to do so would be the end of her career.

But, she hastened to add, her reluctance had nothing to do with him personally.

She loved him.

She wanted to be with him.

But for the moment at least, her career came first.

She hoped he understood.

And to be honest, he didn't.

But he didn't want to lose her either.

So, he was prepared to wait.

For as long as it took.

For her to want to marry him more than she wanted or needed her job.

Because in a roundabout way, through horse shit and piss, he did understand.

If losing his office job was bad, how much worse it must be for her.

Given how much more restricted the opportunities for respectable avenues of work for women outside the home were.

He recalled his mother, after his father died, struggling to find and keep work while taking care of him and his three younger sisters.

How he had given up on his dream of an office job for their sake and taken the first job that offered enough money to see them taken care of.

So, he accepted her terms, and they carried on as they had been.

Living as much as man and wife as she would allow, before putting her on the last train at the end of the day.

She counted the days so she didn't get pregnant, and ruin her life.

Their lives.

All was well for many years.

So well his colleagues and friends started teasing him about making an honest woman of her.

Surely he'd made enough money to set her up comfortably now?

He blushed and stuttered, and they roared with laughter.

He mentioned it once more to Felicia, but she said if anything, her circumstances were such that she was even more reluctant to marry him.

Her career had progressed, she had more responsibility and was making more money.

But her love for him was unchanged, and she hoped he understood.

This time, it felt a little personal.

However, he still loved her.

And if not marrying her was what it took to keep her, then he would not marry her.

Now, it so happened that one day at work, he was walking under the stairs when someone up above dropped an empty crate.

It fell, crashing from floor to floor, and by the time it reached the ground where Tom was walking, it was mostly kindling. Grazing his face as it landed on his shoulder when he didn't back away fast enough.

Yes, it hurt, but he gave his face a quick wash with his handkerchief, thanked his dead parents for keeping him safe, and got back to work.

A few days later, his jaw ached, but he didn't really think much of it.

Just put it down to a little stiffness from the falling crate incident.

But a few days more and his jaw was clenching, and his arms and shoulder were spasming.

He knew something was wrong, and just in case, he wrote an informal will, leaving everything to Felicia.

That afternoon, his back and neck were arching. And a little after that, he was having trouble breathing.

His boss panicked and called an ambulance.

The doctor at the hospital declared it was tetanus.

Which was in those days, a death sentence.

A relatively quick, but very painful death, with nothing available in the way of treatment.

Just a little pain management to keep him more or less comfortable.

Felicia was distraught.

Holding his hand, begging him to get better.

Promising to marry him if he didn't die.

He couldn't say anything in reply, only grin as his face spasmed, and groan as his body arched making his bones creak.

The nurses hustled the horrified Felicia away.

Within fourteen days of being stuck by the remains of the crate he was gone.

Knowing that at least he had provided her with a fully paid-up funeral and life insurances, his savings and bits and pieces of furniture.

Enough that she could, if she wanted to, take a house and live independently of her parents.

As for Felicia, she never once looked at another man.

Whenever she was faced with an important decision, she asked herself, what would Tom do, then acted accordingly.

Knowing life was short and unpredictable, she only ever drank French Champagne, and ate fresh strawberries with cream every summer.

And when the tetanus vaccine was released, she was first in line.

THE END

THE SECRETARIAL SHELTER

When Mr Charles Weatherby of Weatherby & Sons, Inc. first met Miss Felicia Clarke he was impressed by her self-possession.

Sitting in his office, calm, composed and controlled in the hard chair on the other side of his overly large, inherited mahogany desk.

Back straight, hands folded quietly in her lap.

She'd tucked her small bag under the chair as she'd sat down, and it wasn't quite concealed by the fall of her old-fashioned long skirt.

She did not move without purpose during the entire time she was there.

Not a fidget, nor a gesture, not even to uncross and recross her legs.

Not once.

When he thought back, he wasn't entirely convinced she'd even blinked.

Miss Clarke had been referred to him by his good friend Barnaby who thought she might do well as young Mr Sutton's first secretary.

Barnaby was retiring at the end of the year, and he was determined to see his secretary placed somewhere appropriate before he closed his practice.

He couldn't recommend her highly enough and had spoken warmly of her calm competence on more than one occasion.

And of the duplicitous charm she could switch on and off as the situation warranted, such that she'd had the famously brutish industrialist John Sumner eating out of her hand.

A delight to behold Barnaby had said.

Such a shame about her fiancé; dead of tetanus. Very nasty business.

Seemingly, never so much as looked at another man.

Not that anyone was going to want to marry a woman her age, but nonetheless, her status as a dried-up spinster made her more reliable than the young, flighty women who were just looking to marry a lawyer.

But the thing about Miss Clarke that intrigued him the most, was that she watched him watching her.

Like a barn cat honing in, ready to pounce on an unsuspecting small bird or mouse.

She appeared to be assessing his suitability as an employer, and he had the oddest feeling he was disappointing her.

And if she didn't like him, she would refuse his offer of employment, no matter what the capacity.

Somewhat disconcerting that he felt she found him remarkably lacking in some way.

He had of course attempted to bully and hector all the candidates; in the legal profession a secretary is bound to come across many distressed and unhappy clients, and Charles considered it an essential part of a secretary's role to shelter the lawyer in question.

And he had no doubt Mr Sutton would result in many aggrieved parties arriving at her desk.

However, given that her expressionless face and steady gaze was making a man of his age and experience feel like a callow youth, he didn't doubt she would be a formidable barrier to any disgruntled client.

Charles had no idea how long she'd been waiting in reception before she'd reported herself.

She'd arrived so discreetly his own secretary Butler hadn't seen her arrive, so she'd seen at least one young woman depart in tears.

Butler was old school, one of the last of the male secretaries. Didn't in principle approve of women in the office.

Not proper as far as he was concerned.

Perversely, the cooler Miss Clarke's reception, the more Charles was convinced of her suitability.

Butler knocked on the closed door of the office, barely pausing before walking in, carrying a cup of fragrant Earl Grey tea by the saucer to his desk and departing with a sniff.

The shortbread biscuit Charles permitted himself at three o'clock slipped from the saucer to the blotting paper covered desk with a small thud that seemed to reverberate around the room.

Miss Clarke smiled slightly and raised one eyebrow, but otherwise remained still.

Charles almost started to make excuses before remembering who, and where he was.

Besides, he couldn't tell whether she was smiling at his afternoon tea, or the fact she hadn't been offered any.

Miss Clarke was obviously a force to be reckoned with, she'd be wasted on Mr Sutton.

Had she been like that when she was engaged?

A terrifying prospect making him pity the man she as engaged to.

She looked at the overly large man's wristwatch swamping her delicate wrist, then folded herself in half to pick up her bag and stand up in one smooth movement, "if there's nothing further?"

He had to concede there was not, and nodding, "I expect to make a decision shortly, you can expect a letter by the end of next week."

"Then I'll bid you a good day Mr Weatherby," and she was gone.

Not in a lingering haze of strong perfume as the candidate preceding her, after whom they'd had to open and close the windows several times to clear the air.

No doubt he'd need to air his suit thoroughly before he wore it again.

But such was the speed of Miss Clarke's exit, he could have sworn there was a small pop as the displaced air left the loose papers on his desk flapping in her wake.

««« • »»»

Charles struggled through another two interviews before the last candidate left squalling, and it was safe to say they suffered by comparison to Miss Clarke.

All the candidates suffered by comparison to Miss Clarke.

Charles was at a complete loss, not a situation that he was accustomed to.

Butler returned to take Charles' cold tea away.

Surely one secretary could size the others up, why not ask his own for an opinion?

"Stay a minute Butler," he said indicating the chair, "tell me what you think of the candidates."

Butler sat on the edge of the hard chair, shoulders up around his head, and cleared his throat.

Then said nothing.

He swallowed, Adam's apple bouncing, and cleared his throat again, "you recall my son moved to Manchester to take up a clerking position in a cotton factory?"

"Yes of course, how is he doing?"

"Doing well Sir. Got married, and we just heard they're pregnant."

"That's excellent news, congratulations."

Charles was starting to get an idea of where the conversation was heading.

"Um... Mrs Butler wants to move up there to be nearby, and... Er..."

"She wants you to resign and go too?"

Butler's shoulders dropped as if he was glad to have it out in the open at last, "ah... Yes Sir."

"I see. And I can't persuade you to stay?"

Butler shrugged, "you know what they say Sir, happy wife happy life."

"I see," though never having been married, Charles didn't see at all.

"So the way I see it, the only one of them's any good is the quiet one, Miss Clarke, and she's too good for Sutton.

"You should hire her for yourself, and the young one..." he looked up at the ceiling struggling to remember the name, "Miss Evans for Mr Sutton; the two young'uns can muddle through together.

"Miss Clarke ought to be able to help Miss Evans get through some of it, the rest she'll have to learn on her own."

"This coming from the man who doesn't think women belong in offices?"

Butler sighed. "My wife tells me I should move with the times, but I'm not sure I want to. Manchester is more conservative, so I think I'll do well there."

"I understand," though to be honest, Charles didn't have a frame of reference for that either.

It wasn't that Charles was selfish or self-involved, just that he tended to get caught up in the cases he was working on.

And so it came as somewhat of a surprise to find that Butler had gone and Miss Clarke had more or less seamlessly taken over his duties.

"I should have sent him away with something," Charles fretted.

"You did, you gave him a gold watch."

"Did I? Surely I would remember if I had."

"You were buried in the Sweet case at the time, so given his loyalty and length of service, I purchased the watch and had it engraved on your behalf."

Charles stood up and blustered, "I should have been consulted."

Miss Clarke sat down, "you were. Do you not recall I offered you the catalogue to choose? And asked what sentiment the engraving should be?"

"I—

"Ah... Yes... I apologise.

"Is it not very odd he didn't thank me?"

She stood up to rifle through the top layers of papers on his desk for Butler's letter, "it's here. I'll bring you some tea and leave you to read it."

He sat heavily in his chair, raised the letter to look at it, and thought how awfully he seemed to have behaved.

Miss Clarke returned with his tea, and this time two biscuits, seeming to understand he needed a little extra something.

Charles read the letter, somewhat reassured to find Butler had only just left.

That he appreciated the minimum of fuss, not being one to socialise with the lower employees.

And had appreciated the watch and the warmth of the gesture, and would always treasure it.

Charles sighed.

Then put his coat and hat on, telling Miss Clarke he was going for a walk.

"I've freed your afternoon, so don't feel obliged to return," she said.

So he didn't.

《《 • 》》

He found a subtle difference to the offices when he returned the next day.

As if someone had opened all the windows to let some fresh air in.

And cleaned them all to let more light in too.

Miss Clarke had installed some kind of yellow flowers on her desk and they certainly brightened up the place.

She gave him a moment to remove his hat and coat, and reorient himself before bringing in a tray with two cups of tea, thereby giving him to understand they were playing by her rules from now on.

He signed some letters and orders, they talked through some matters she could progress, and she laid out his schedule for the day.

As he looked past her and out the window onto a dreary day, he noticed a jug of water and four glasses on the credenza by the window, and wondered why he hadn't thought of that before.

A little later, when she ushered his first appointment in, he offered them some water and she winked at him.

And a little later, with another client, she brought a tea tray with a pot of tea and two cups by which he understood that this client needed a little more time and attention.

On another occasion, there was even a plate of biscuits to accompany the tea.

He understood her level of client care was a clue, guiding him towards his next action.

Not to say that she was anything other than professional, but as Barnaby had suggested, she was able to chop and change her approach according to what each client needed.

And so, as a little thank you, he started bringing her flowers on Monday mornings.

Just a small token bunch at first, but as the years progressed, the more elaborate the arrangements became, until after many more years it became necessary to acquire a dedicated table to sit them on.

Every Friday evening, Miss Clark donated the flowers somewhere or another; Charles told himself it was not appropriate to question her on the issue.

But the truth was, he was a little afraid to; better she donate them than throw them in the bin.

Over time, it became clear that she could get to the heart of a matter - very often what clients said was not the issue at all.

As if a doctor, she saw through the symptoms to the cause, and generally by the time someone came pursuing legal solutions, there were a lot of symptoms.

That's not to say that she knew the Law intimately, more that she understood people, and would often lead him down previously unexplored avenues of inquiry.

He started to get a reputation of case resolution before court proceedings commenced, and correspondingly, more clients who paid their less expensive bills more promptly.

Charles took to offering her a little sherry at the end of each week to celebrate their successes.

And it wasn't much later she relaxed enough to suggest he could call her Felicia outside of office hours.

And of course, he asked her to call him Charles.

There is no doubt that over time, the relationship between secretary and employer can be intimate.

People don't snigger about "the wife at the office" for no reason.

And very often a man spends more time at work with his secretary than he does at home with his wife.

Especially where there are rambunctious children at home too.

There is a kind of forced familiarity, an unintentional confidentiality that comes about because they spend so much time together.

This intensity can easily be confused for love.

And so it was for Charles.

He'd been working closely with Miss Clarke for many years when he attempted to kiss her after too many sherries one Friday evening.

«« • »»

It's tempting to say that Miss Clarke returned his affection, that they got married and lived Happy Ever After.

I know you, dear reader, would like that, and would possibly feel much more satisfied if I did.

But Real Life isn't like the kind of Fairy Stories we tell little girls hoping they'll grow up to be empty-headed and biddable beauties.

Real Life requires ongoing calculation and assessment of your options.

Would Miss Clarke be better off surrendering her independence and marrying some guy?

Could he possibly take better care of her than she could herself?

Was her resting bitch face a better deterrent than the threat of an irate husband?

That's not to say that Miss Clarke wasn't tempted now and then, but the more you keep your own company, the less you want to share it.

Happy Ever After doesn't take account of washing your husband's stinky socks and underpants.

Nor his coming home drunk again, passing out on the doorstep leaving you to manhandle him up the stairs and into your bed.

That he expects you to keep to his schedule, showing no regard to your own.

So when your own Fairy Tale presents itself to you, consider whether you might be falling for the propaganda.

Think about the downsides as well as the up.

«« • »»

So poor Charles had, after too many sherries, attempted to kiss Felicia one Friday evening.

Luckily, he hadn't had so many sherries he didn't detect her sudden rigidity.

And came to the uncomfortable truth that he had misconstrued their familiarity for love.

And in that instant, he weighed up his options; a task men seem more able for.

He now knew marriage was not one of them.

He was greatly tempted to ignore the situation; pretend it had never happened.

But he correctly thought if he didn't acknowledge his transgression, he would never see her again.

These calculations took mere fractions of a second.

Mortified, he let her go as he stumbled back.

"I was out of line," he blurted, "I apologise. It won't happen again."

She stood up, placing her glass on his desk, and examining his face at great length.

For such a long time he was worried he'd be frozen in place forever.

Seemingly satisfied, she said, "then I forgive you," and left the room.

As he put a hand on his heart, attempting to slow its pace, he heard her collect her things and leave.

He sat heavily in his chair, hoping she wasn't the kind of woman who held grudges, though he'd never had an inkling she might be.

Charles fretted all weekend.

《《 • 》》

Monday morning arrived, and he bought a simple bunch of carnations into the office because he knew they were his favourite flower.

As usual, she thanked him, and gave him a moment to remove his hat and coat before she brought in the tea tray.

And as usual, they discussed his schedule, other related matters and he signed the letters and orders.

As she collected the papers together, he cleared his throat and said, "about Friday—"

"There's no need to say another word, it's as forgotten as if it never happened."

And true to her word, it really was as if it had never happened.

So much so, that many years after that, when he took the memory out and looked at it, it seemed like the fevered dream of his over-active imagination.

«« • »»

When at last Charles retired, he, like Barnaby all those years ago, fretted about what to do with Felicia.

And tried to shop her around to his friends in the legal profession, but time had moved on.

She had no qualifications, wasn't fond of typewriters that moved faster than her, and not completely sure about those new-fangled computers.

He broached the subject with her, and she surprised him.

She would retire herself.

Take trips to visit her sisters in New Zealand and Australia.

Do all those other things she'd been waiting for the available time to do.

«« • »»

Their last day together passed uneventfully.

It wasn't much more than a formality.

All the files were fully written up and dispatched to their new owners.

His office was clean and empty, ready for its new owner.

They took one last long lunch, at the end of which she shook his hand and walked away.

Charles Weatherby never saw Felicia Clark again, but often wondered how she was faring.

THE END

MY LUCKY CUSTOMER

Erol stood on the street, key in hand, admiring the tiny shop he'd just signed the lease on.

Something he couldn't have conceived of as a boy during the war.

He'd barely thought past the very next minute; where to hide, where to get food, and whatever happened to the rest of his family.

Arriving in England and getting permission to stay was a miracle.

For years he'd worked five part-time, casual jobs, living week to week in a small room in a rooming house, eating leftovers from the plates at the restaurant he washed dishes in.

Saving all his money for this day.

The building itself was at least 200 years old, and the London yellow bricks had achieved a fairly uniform coating of black dust he couldn't do anything about.

It was the same shade as all the other buildings around it so it didn't stand out.

But the store frontage did.

Painted orange of all things.

So cheerful against the gloom he'd fallen in love with it.

He found the colour comforting as well, though he couldn't remember a time when something orange made him feel safe.

The London skies weren't as bright or clear as those he'd grown up with. Even in midsummer the sunshine painted the whole town in a muted watercolour grey wash.

The orange Edwardian style frontage surrounded two glass windows and a half glass door with kick plates at street level.

They were sandwiched between two plain, modern blue doors either side leading to the first and second story flats respectively.

The windows had a thin coat of whitewash, presumably to deter squatters, and he hoped it wouldn't be hard to get off; that the windows would actually clean.

He'd need all the light he could force into the shop!

He turned the key and opened the door, faced with a single open room, strewn with rubbish and in dire need of cleaning.

Though perhaps it wouldn't seem so bad once he'd washed the white off the windows.

Best of all, through a door to his right, stairs to a tiny basement.

There was no natural light from the street, so the zoning didn't permit residential, but as it included a rudimentary bathroom and kitchen, he planned to live there anyway.

He'd need all the hours of the day to get set up, and make his tiny business a success.

Erol wanted to immediately start ordering stock and fittings for the store, and perhaps one or two small pieces of furniture for the basement.

But first, logic required cleaning the place so he could move in.

He locked the door, and walked down to the DIY store, to buy some cleaning products and a measuring tape.

And then a few hours later, back to the DIY store to buy a small ladder, some paint and bits and pieces for the small repairs required.

Then later still, back to his digs to shower and change for his shift at the restaurant.

Only after his five hour shift did he manage to get to his computer to the second hand store supply company he'd bookmarked to order the furniture.

The best thing about ordering second hand, was next day delivery!

Or given it was very early in the morning, the day after.

Only then did he sleep.

Then packed his bags, turned in his rooming house keys, and set off for his new life without looking back.

Later that evening, he stood outside his orange store, surrounded by his bags and packages, enjoying the moment.

His very own tiny store!

"Are you lost?" a woman's voice asked.

He turned to see a middle aged woman wearing an old-fashioned navy blue skirt suit, carrying a bulging shopping bag over one arm.

She didn't seem to notice a lock of greying dark hair had escaped her bun and was twisted around her neck.

She looked tired. Worn out.

Erol smiled, hoping to lighten her load, seeing as she had stopped to ask if he was all right.

"No Ma'am, I'm admiring my new shop."

She put her bag down and turned to look at the empty shop. "Well, it certainly looks very clean. What will you be selling."

"It's a convenience store."

"Good choice. There's not much of that around here. If you stock pints of milk, half loaves of wholemeal, and Silk Cut in packs of ten I'll stop by every day."

"Thank you Ma'am, I'll certainly do that."

She smiled and picked up her bag, "when will you open?"

"Next week."

"Then I'll see you then."

He watched her walk past the next couple of shops before turning into the first street on the left.

He hoped she didn't have far to go, she looked dead on her feet.

When he got back inside, he took his bags down stairs, and came back with his string of lucky charms.

During the war, he'd given up on gods, and started reciting a list of every single piece of good luck that happened to him.

Once he got a little more settled, he started buying lucky charms to represent them. Erol figured they'd work as well as prayers, if not better.

Though in a way, they became a kind of string of prayer beads as he touched each charm while reciting the list.

It had grown into a good, thick string of charms, so it seemed to be working. He'd have to find another two charms to add now. One for the shop, and one for the lady.

He dragged the ladder over, and hung it from a hook in the ceiling. Like a shop bell; it would chime when someone opened the door.

Hopefully multiplying his blessings every time someone did.

He opened and shut the door a couple of times to make it ring.

It was going to be great.

But in the meantime, he had dishes to wash.

«« • »»

The next day, he was up early, restlessly pacing, waiting for the furniture to arrive.

To calm his nerves, in what would become part of his morning routine, he took his standing brush with the blue plastic pan and swept the street directly in front of his shop.

He heard footsteps trotting down the path and looked up to see yesterday's navy-suited woman walking down the street in the same blue suit, or one very like it.

"Good morning Ma'am," he said as she neared.

"And good morning to you," she replied, nodding as she walked past.

He watched her walk further down the street, thinking she must work very long hours.

No wonder she was so tired when she walked back again.

He wondered where she worked.

Before too long he'd invented a life for her, working in the City at a merchant bank or some such; always rushed off her feet.

He hoped they appreciated her, and treated her like the Lady he knew she was.

He sighed, thinking and hoping, that soon he'd be rushed off his feet as well.

Having swept the footpath, he went back inside, sitting on the floor with his laptop, to start ordering stock. Including milk in pints, bread in half loaves, but was disappointed for find he could only order cigarettes in packs of twenty.

Almost before he'd finished, the furniture started arriving, and he spent the day arranging, and rearranging the shelves and fridge around the walls, and carrying and arranging his living accommodations downstairs.

The local women and children watched him working, but ignored him as he greeted them.

He found the staring a little unnerving, but consoled himself that he had one regular customer already.

Much later, he was sitting on the doorstep, resting before heading to the restaurant when his navy-suited lady walked up to him, carrying a bulging shopping bag.

"How is it coming along?" she asked.

"Very well Ma'am. Some of the stock will start arriving in the morning."

"That's exciting for you."

"Yes."

"Well, I'll let you get on," she said, and kept walking.

Such a lady.

«« • »»

The days flew past.

Stock came in, he arranged it in the shelves, flattened the boxes and packed them up to go out with the rubbish.

The navy suited lady walked down the road in the morning, and back up in the evening.

He was always outside ready to greet her.

He notified the restaurant he was leaving, but worked right up until the night before his shop opened.

«« • »»

The night before he opened, Erol was so excited, he barely slept a wink.

Driven out of bed early by nervous anticipation, he almost prayed for success, but recalled himself just in time, reciting his good luck list instead.

He got out of bed and climbed the stairs to check the store layout, one last time.

Were the right products in the right place?

Would it promote a good flow of traffic around the space?

Just about the time he was about to go mad with doubt, he heard a van slow outside, then two distinct thuds as the newspapers were thrown out, followed by a roar as the van sped off to its next stop.

He dragged the papers in and arranged them on the counter.

And then to calm himself, he started a new routine; dusting the cheap light fixtures hanging from the ceiling, then moving onto the cigarette displays and the cards of lighters, cheap toys and other bits and bobs hanging from the walls.

Moving onto the shelves and the goods on them, wiping down the refrigerated units, and spraying the counter with cleaner.

Finally, sweeping the floor. Edging his small broom under the wooden shelves, sweeping the dust, loose hairs and fluff into the pan.

And as the time of the blue-suited lady approached, out onto the street to sweep off the footpath.

"Good morning," she said, "are you open?"

"Yes Ma'am," and scurried to open the door for her, "what can I help you with?"

She walked past him into the store, taking a quick look around before meeting him at the counter.

"It's looking good, you should do well with what you've got," which was a load of his mind.

She continued, "I'll take The Guardian and a pack of Silk Cut."

He folded the paper in half, topped it with the cigarettes, apologising for the law having changed and not being permitted to sell packs of ten.

"I'm sorry," she said, "I'd forgotten." She handed over a £5 note, adding, "keep the change."

"Thank you Ma'am."

She turned to the door, then looked back at him, "what time do you shut?"

He smiled, "about the same time I see you walking back every day."

"Then see you later alligator," she said with a wink as she walked out the door.

He listened to the chiming charms, and grinned.

That his first customer should be his navy-suit lady was good luck.

That she told him to keep the change made him want to frame the note for more good luck.

«« • »»

Though by the end of the day, he was feeling as though his luck had run out.

He did not see one single other customer all day.

When his navy-suited lady arrived that evening, he was despondent.

"Cheer up," she said, placing her bread, milk and a tin of baked beans on the counter, "you're here now, they'll get here too. Just as soon as they start running out of things."

He mumbled something shameful and she laughed.

"It's only the first day! Half the street hasn't even figured out you're here yet. Why don't you put a poster in the window offering some opening week discounts? I'm sure that will bring people in."

And when he thought about it, that wasn't a bad idea.

He decided on discounting the bread and milk as it wasn't the kind of thing he could hold over for long.

«« • »»

Over the next few days, as customers started trickling in, the navy-suited lady encouraging him to start thinking about his little shop on a larger level.

It was more than just his little shop, it was a part of a community. And if he wanted to make a living, (and he did), he needed to make it his community.

His community was mostly the white English people who lived in the surrounding streets.

The few Asians were outliers, and he could stock a few things for them, but he didn't want to be seen as an Asian supermarket.

For his shop to be a success, he needed to stock the particular goods his community needed.

He made time to walk about the estate, looking at the flats and houses they lived in, and smelling the foods they cooked.

He visited the nearby stores and closest supermarkets where they might be shopping.

He even looked at the rubbish in the streets to see what he could learn from that.

When the children started coming in to spend their pocket money, he asked them about their favourite ice creams, crisps and sweets and made sure he ordered them in.

As their mother's started coming in, what sizes and brands of products they preferred.

And the men, what cigarettes and alcohol.

The whole thing terrified him; asking total strangers what they wanted, but he understood the need to get to know his people.

Some of them didn't take it well; "sod off you paki-bastard go back to where you came from and mind your own business."

But he learned and grew, got better at asking, and started getting better answers "oh, I've got five kids so always the biggest boxes of cereal."

And he remembered it all, "how are you and your five kids - I've got that cereal here for whenever you need it."

And through it all, the navy-suited woman was there, his first customer in the morning, and the last at night.

Offering her little bits of advice.

Consoling him on the rude customers.

And congratulating him on the best.

«« • »»

As the years progressed, his store became a place his community could rely on. He always had just what they needed, and nothing more.

Throughout it all, the navy-suited woman continued to be his best customer.

His ideal customer, about whom he remembered all the little snippets of information he learned about her.

That she walked to Kings Cross Station in the morning rather than Caledonian Road because it was easier for her to get on the tube.

After work she walked home via the supermarket, and when he discovered how many ready meals she ate, he started stocking her favourites for her convenience.

And after advertising their introduction with a poster in the window, was surprised at how popular they were with other customers.

As the local children grew older and ruder, she spoke to them, then marched them back inside to apologise to him.

Sometimes their parents would come in later to apologise as well.

It turned out she worked for a lawyer, and rarely made it out for lunch, so he started stocking ready made sandwiches.

Similarly, with a poster in the window, he started selling more of them too.

For every small change he made for her convenience, he was rewarded with a gain from his other customers.

«« • »»

One day, decades after he'd first met her, she came to tell him she was moving away.

"I have cancer. I'm moving North to be closer to my niece."

"Oh my," he said, "I'm so sorry. Is there anything I can do to to help."

She laughed; a strangely chilling sound, "there's nothing anyone can do now."

"I'm so sorry."

And he was. He wished there was something he could do.

He looked around the shop, trying to see something he could give her.

She turned to go.

"Wait!"

She turned back, watching him dash for the step ladder.

He carefully took the bulky string of lucky charms down, and offered it to her. "I think you might need this luck more than me."

Her hands dipped with the weight of the charm threaded strings.

"I can't take this," she said.

"Ma'am—"

"Felicia," she corrected, "it occurs to me that after more than twenty years, I haven't told you my name."

He smiled, not mentioning it had in fact been thirty-four years, seven months, and fifteen days.

He placed his hands under hers, supporting the weight of the charms in hers, "Felicia, consider for a moment, that over that time, I have taken your luck."

"Not at all. I have been lucky to have such a dedicated shopkeeper here in you."

"Almost all my luck has been yours," he said, and recited his list of good luck, counting the charms, stopping as he got to the first day he met her, showing her how much longer and thicker the string had become since he'd met her.

"Please take this," he said, putting one hand on his heart, "it's all in here anyway."

"All right," she said as she pulled the charm he'd bought when they first met from the strings. "Take this, and start a new string."

"I will," he said, clutching it so hard it bit into his hand.

"Good luck then."

"And you."

The door opened and closed silently.

He did not watch her walk away.

And he never saw her again.

But if he'd been a praying man, he would have prayed for her.

THE END

STRANGER DANGER

Once upon a time, a long, long time ago, a stranger changed the course of my life forever.

For the better.

I really don't know what would have become of me if I hadn't met her.

For that matter, I don't even like to speculate.

Never before, or since, has someone had that level of impact.

I wish I knew her name, so I could thank her. Though I suppose she was old at the time, and it's been decades now.

She's probably dead.

But, it's such a shame she'll never know how much she changed my life after we met.

I think I was about fifteen at the time, sitting alone on a seat in the dog park.

The seat was hidden in a small copse of grevilleas or hakeas or something, right up the back.

Completely obscured from the gravel path winding through and around the park.

And everyone else in the park.

Or so I thought.

Outside the sun blazed, but it was cool and dark within.

A breeze had blown up outside, but inside the copse, it was quiet and still.

Aside from the soft swish of the leaves brushing against each other.

If you closed your eyes and used your imagination, it sounded like gentle waves washing up on the shore.

Though being sheltered, and in amongst the scratchy, snarly bushes, it was also alive with orange and grey spinebills flitting from branch-to-branch drinking nectar from the red and orange flowers.

Moving so fast they were just bright flashes of colour.

Chirping and tweeting as they caught up on the gossip.

It was the perfect place to hide.

At least it was if you weren't allergic to bee stings.

The drone as they floated from honey-scented flower to honey-scented flower was strangely relaxing given the danger.

And making me drowsy.

Only rarely would a dog bravely push through the bushes and bees to the inside, which had grown littered with tennis balls in varying stages of decomposition.

Sometimes I took pity on them and threw the balls over the top to a melody of delighted barks.

And sometimes I just listened to their disappointed howls.

The copse was a retreat of a kind.

I'm sure at one point the seat was out in the open before the bushes grew up around it. But it sat, seemingly forgotten by everyone.

It was the one place where I knew I was so unlikely as to see anyone as to be the perfect hideaway.

I used it a lot in those days.

Just tucked my knees up so I could rest my cheek against them and closed my eyes.

Listening to the birds and bees, and the odd car back-firing as the world carried on as usual outside.

As I enjoyed the warm, scented closeness, it was almost as if the bushes embraced me.

Kept me safe from the real world outside.

The scratchy bushes were the perfect bird sanctuary, and so it was full of birds.

I usually sat so still they shared the seat, pausing for a moment between snacks.

And going by the amount of guano, they used it a lot while I wasn't there as well.

Guano dripping down the back of the seat. Guano on the front, the arms, and the seat.

Probably more Guano on the seat than in the park itself.

Dogs included.

I read somewhere that they used to mine guano in Australia.

Mined so much of it they ruined all the coastal bird habitats. Drove the birds away from their nesting places.

Not that they cared much about that kind of thing in those days. Not like these days.

Usually I carried a large spotted handkerchief with me everywhere I went, because I'd read somewhere that large spots made you happy.

And in those days, we couldn't afford to buy tissues. Or handkerchiefs for that matter; I saved up my Christmas and birthday money to buy them, and I have never come across anyone else who did that too.

But I'd left the house in such a rush I'd left my handkerchief, and everything else that was useful there.

Including protection from the bushes in the form of jeans and a long-sleeved shirt.

So I couldn't even cover the damn seat with something to protect my clothes.

I just sat there in my tattered shorts and ripped singlet, covered in stinging scratches.

Because at the time I didn't feel like I deserved to sit anywhere other than in the guano.

Actually, let's call it what it is - shit.

I didn't feel like I deserved to sit anywhere other than in the shit.

Deep layers of stinking, wet shit.

You can probably guess I was in low spirits.

My parents had been fighting again, I don't know what about, but I assumed it had to be me.

Because I was an only child, and we didn't have any pets, so what else could it have been?

Parents are often obtuse.

And I just couldn't bear it anymore.

I snuck out while they were glaring at each other, and hightailed it to the park.

Crawling into the copse on my hands and knees because the branches were about as long as they were high and it was easier than forcing my way though upright.

As I said, the close atmosphere was like a soft, warm embrace.

Comforting.

I started crying.

Not the quiet, dignified kind you see in the movies, with tears slipping quietly down your face, but the kind of violet sobs that make an ugly noise as they wrack your whole body.

"Are you alright in there honey?" a voice asked.

I tried to be quiet so she'd go away, but at the same time, the concern in her voice made me cry harder and uglier.

So loud and self-absorbed I didn't hear her trying to get through the copse until she was in.

"Nice place you have here."

I was so surprised I started hiccupping.

The woman was old.

I thought she was must be more than one hundred, but I was young. She probably wasn't any older than sixty or seventy.

And seeing as she was at least one hundred, I was impressed she'd braved the bushes.

Though she was wearing dark blue jeans with a crease ironed down the front and a white and blue striped button-down shirt fastened at the round collar, so she was fairly well scratch proofed.

Some of her white hair had escaped from her bun and curled around her neck.

She offered me a large, pure white handkerchief with an F embroidered in blue on the corner.

I sniffed and shook my head; I knew they were precious things.

"Nonsense," she said waving it, "I have tonnes of them."

I suppose she understood I couldn't wipe my nose on my sleeve because I didn't have one.

Hesitantly, I took it.

The fabric was thick and finely woven; it was clearly expensive, yet she was offering it to a complete stranger.

A child at that.

"Blow," she said.

I looked at the handkerchief, and then at her, flicking her fingers towards me, urging me to use it.

It was like blowing my nose on a cloud.

"That's better," she said and made to sit on the other end of the seat.

"No!"

She didn't frown like my mother would have, merely raised an eyebrow in query.

"It's dirty."

"Ah," she sat down anyway, "it'll wash."

This was as unexpected as if she had taken a bath in guano.

My mother didn't like it when I got dirty.

She was always on about keeping clean, and respectable, and what would the neighbours think.

If she thought she had even the smallest speck of dust on her clothes she'd change them.

The woman crossed her legs, and glanced at me, but didn't say anything further.

Just looked out at what would have been the rest of the park if she could see through the shrubs.

Or maybe she was watching the birds.

And I didn't say anything either.

We sat quietly for a long time while I harried the rolled edges of the handkerchief.

Or at least it seemed like a long time, but I suppose it was only a couple of minutes.

She pulled a small KitKat from her pocket, sliced it open with a fingernail, snapped it in half and offered one to me.

I barely paused before I took it.

I suppose I should have been concerned about stranger danger, but she'd already offered me her handkerchief.

And a chocolate bar was nowhere near as special as a handkerchief.

Though I did wait until she'd taken a bite of her half before I nibbled at mine.

Trying to make it last.

My mother didn't believe much in chocolate either.

That's not to say I didn't love my mother, because I did.

It's just that she could be...

Well...

Difficult.

We found out later she was bipolar, which didn't make her any less difficult, but easier to deal with once we knew what was going on.

And she started taking the medication.

We ate our snack in a more or less comfortable silence.

And after a while, she asked again, "Are you alright?"

"Um, yes."

"You ran in here so fast I almost didn't believe I'd seen you."

I smiled a straight lipped smile, imagining something like The Flash streaking through the park, a blur of rainbow colour behind me.

"I was in a hurry."

"Yes, I could see that."

"My Mum..."

We sat in silence a while longer as I thought about whether I should say anything or not.

Mum didn't like it when I told tales about her.

Or at least she called them tales.

Now she's gone, I expect she was worried someone would call Child Services and I'd be taken away from her.

But you know what they say, dead men tell no tales, and I will never know now what she was thinking.

The lady waited, not saying anything, examining her fingernails.

"Sometimes we don't agree," I finally said, which seemed safe enough.

"My mother and I didn't agree at all either," the woman said, "we were too much alike in many ways."

I tried to decide whether I was like her, "I can't see it."

"I imagine when you get older you'll see it better."

I grunted noncommittally and turned my face up to the sun.

She chuckled.

I glared at her, but she was looking inwards, not at me.

"I've done so much more than my mother could ever have imagined."

"Like what?"

"I've visited every single continent, even Antarctica and the North Pole."

My jaw dropped.

"And I visited all the major art galleries from the Guggenheim in New York, to the Louvre in Paris, to the Mori Art Museum in Tokyo."

"I like art," I said, "it's my favourite subject. I want to be an artist when I grow up."

"Good for you!"

"Mum says that's ridiculous. That I'll never make a living from it and I should aim at working in a shop."

The woman smothered a snort.

I was shocked.

It had never occurred to me that Mum could be wrong about something.

"Hon, you absolutely can make a good living from art; it's not all painting pictures you know. You could work in advertising, publishing, or architecture and that's just a start.

"You can get jobs in all kinds of industries! Just check what you need to get into art college and you're on your way."

It seemed too easy.

"I'm not sure Mum would agree to that."

"Well, I can't predict what she'll say, but would you like to know what I'd do?"

I looked again at her clothes and her expensive handkerchief still clutched in my fist.

Clearly, she was successful at whatever it was she did; wearing expensive clothes and travelling all over the world.

"Okay."

"First, you need to work out all the reasons your mother won't agree with you, and then you need to research all the answers.

"And then when she tells you it's too expensive, you can tell her exactly how much it will cost, and how you might get a scholarship. And how much you can expect to earn your first year out.

"That kind of thing."

And when the woman put it like that, it was that simple.

All I had to do was find out when and where, and I'd be golden.

But I guess she could read the doubt written all over my face.

"I bet you think you're all grown up, but you've only lived a tiny fraction of your life."

Still, I frowned.

"Let's say you've lived one lifetime so far, all things being equal, you've another seven or eight lifetimes to go."

I counted out my lifetimes - she was talking about ninety years.

"That's a long time to be a shop-girl when you want to be an artist."

I tried to imagine how long ninety years was when I could barely get my head around the long, summer school holidays.

I don't remember how the rest of the conversation went, but I remember when I offered her the handkerchief back, she told me to keep it.

As a good luck charm.

I ran home, got changed, and ran to the library where the librarian helped me to research my questions.

And a few weeks later when I had the answers, I started talking to my parents about going to technical college to learn graphic design.

And I started college the next year.

Since then, I've designed all kinds of things; magazines, wallpapers, logos. You name it, I've probably designed it.

I never forgot the lady's technique for getting what I want.

I've used it for work, and in my personal life; to negotiate pay rises and contracts, as well as who does the dishes, and cleans the kitty litter tray.

That's why I framed what remains of the handkerchief, and hung it in my office to remind me where I came from.

And to pay attention to the kind advice of strangers.

To embrace the danger of the unknown.

I am, and forever will be, grateful for her intercession.

THE END

BEST FRIENDS FOREVER

I should really start this story in the beginning. When I first met Felicia rather than at the end when I last saw her, before...

Well, before her funeral.

But given there was a break of about fifty years between the dates, and for forty-five of them, I'd lost contact.

I'd married Danforth, a nice enough man, and he'd taken me back to his home town up North.

I quit work, had a family, and just didn't get around to replying to her last letter.

At the time she was everything I wanted to be.

But after a while, I simply forgot about her.

Now I think back and wonder how that was even possible.

She and I were quite the thing at Mungo's Secretarial College.

Along with...

What's his name?

It's on the tip of my tongue.

T...

Th...

Thad? Theo? Thomas?

Thomas, that was it.

Tom.

I'd always thought she'd marry him, but apparently, her father was a bit of a layabout and her family was as good as destitute while she was growing up and she vowed that she would never be beholden to a man.

Or dependent on a man's...

What was it she called it?

I can't remember, but I do think she really loved him.

Tom, this is.

And anyway, I think she wanted to take care of her mother, and if she got married, she'd have to give up work and take care of her husband.

I tell you; he had the patience of a saint that man.

Such a shame he died of tetanus; I mean who could ever have imagined that?

Awful way to die.

She gave up on God after that- just a bigger, badder man she said.

Perhaps he's waiting for her at the Pearly Gates.

More the fool him then, he'll be waiting for all eternity because she's not going to get there.

Nuts. Just nuts.

Anyway, where was I?

When I got married, I wouldn't say there were fireworks at the beginning, but he's been a good provider and really, what woman could ask for more than that?

So that being said, I did my duty by my husband too.

When he turned his attentions to his secretary, if you know what I mean, I was quite frankly glad to be rid of it.

And when he left me for her it was hilarious.

She was not much older than our daughter, and as you probably know, life with a young woman in the house can be quite turbulent.

Quite frankly, I can't believe he forgot that.

Not to mention that young women these days are somewhat more liberated than us, and he ended up washing both their clothes, cooking food for the two of them and tidying up after her.

I almost felt sorry for him when he came snivelling back to me, though I was under no illusions that he felt anything for me.

Just longed for the calm, easy life I provided him.

So, let's just say we renegotiated the terms of our marriage, and he increased my housekeeping by several thousand and stopped querying my expenditure quite so thoroughly.

Win-win all around, isn't that what they say you should aim for?

And in a way, this was what led me to meeting Felicia again.

I'd packed my big travel handbag with supplies, and we caught the train to London for Danforth's cancer treatment.

And my goodness the whole place was dreary.

Perhaps I've become a Northerner now, but it seemed all gloom to me.

Gloomy London sky, gloomy London hospital, gloomy hospital waiting room.

Perhaps when they're new, waiting rooms are bright and fresh, but after a point, patient fatigue and illness seeps into the walls and floor, coating them with a kind of grey misery.

Or perhaps it's generations of Nurse Ratched live-alikes.

I like to think I have absolutely no psychic ability whatsoever, but even I felt the load on my shoulders gain at least ten stone as I walked through the hospital door.

I sat in the scruffy waiting room and eased my stiff neck by stretching it as far back as I could make it go, then rolled it backwards and forwards against my shoulders.

It was the kind of sore neck you get when you've been hunching your shoulders too long.

The kind of dull throbbing soreness you get when you're stressed out, as the young things like to say.

I tried not to sigh, not to take a deep breath of the refrigerated, recycled and reconditioned air. Perfumed, as it was, with a strange and unpleasant mix of sharp pure alcohol, dirt and antiseptic floor cleaner.

Plus, a hint of urine, if not from Danforth slumping next to me, then presumably someone else in the waiting room.

I have one good eye thanks to cataract surgery last year, and I need a hearing aid, but somehow my sense of smell is sharper than ever.

Had I grown up at a different time, and in France, I'm sure I would've apprenticed as a Nose for a Perfume House instead of attending Mungo's.

Then again, maybe my nose isn't sharper, maybe it's just that I've had more exposure to different scents.

I could probably trace my life through the scents.

Wood polish, old books and cigar smoke when I started work at Father's practise.

Then fresh paper, ink and typewriter ribbons at Mungo's evening classes twice a week.

Fresh mown lawn, lavender and hot dirt when I lost my virginity. To a stranger who smelled of cigarettes, diesel fuel, and sticky date pudding.

Those were the days.

When I was a new adult, unchaperoned, set loose on the world.

I wonder a little bit, what would have become of me if Father had chosen a different secretarial college and I hadn't met Felicia.

I certainly wouldn't have lost my virginity to a stranger, found myself pregnant, or set on Danforth as a suitable father.

Poor Danforth, perhaps he would have met a nicer, kinder woman than me.

Nonetheless, there we were. Three young people (counting Tom), out on the town.

Smoking, drinking, staying out late.

Father didn't approve, said I would come to a bad end, and he was right about that, though not the bad end he was thinking about.

You may not believe it, talking to me now, but I was shy and naive. Everything was new and exciting, and I felt very daring as I eased into my life of duplicity.

Felicia on the other hand was worldly and a bit jaded. I wonder now, what she saw that made her so thoroughly grown up at such a young age.

The way she handled Tom...

Stringing him along all those years.

Though I suppose she strung me along as well.

Felicia glowed with something worldly and cosmopolitan.

Like I imagine the apple that poisoned Sleeping Beauty. Something enticing, seemingly wholesome, and glossy; an enchanting mask hiding the bad seed within.

Who am I kidding - Tom and I, we were both smitten.

She was the one that took us to the club where I met the stranger.

She encouraged me to drink the cocktail the stranger bought me.

She encouraged me to live a little, to dance and kiss the stranger.

And then she left me, taking Tom with her. Left me to the tender ministrations of the stranger.

Whose name I never knew.

How different would my life have been if I had known his name...

And how to contact him.

Still.

You have to move on, don't you?

I used her tricks to snare Danforth.

Stalking him through Father's firm, tricking him into sleeping with me, deceiving him over his paternity (they do say there's one born every minute for a reason).

Allowing him to take the fall with Father for deflowering his daughter.

Quick registry office marriage.

Following him into banishment.

Though moving to his home town did give me the opportunity to create the fiction of love at first sight, a whirlwind romance, happily ever after.

To reinvent myself as a kinder, more understanding woman.

With my own bad seed hidden deeply inside.

So, there I was, in the waiting room with Danforth.

Waiting for a nurse to come get him, and to an extent, waiting for him to die.

When I smelled something like the smell of Mungo's Secretarial College. Fountain pen ink and fresh paper.

Though the nurse called Danforth's name just that minute, and I forgot about it.

Too busy helping him up and supporting him as he walked towards the nurses' station where a male nurse took over and helped him through the door to the treatment room where I could not follow.

And then I was left to my own devices for six hours until it was time to collect him and take him to the hotel I'd booked.

He's always ill that first night so I don't like to take the train straight home.

Besides, I don't enjoy cleaning up the mess, so it's much better when he's closer to a bathroom when he's vomiting or got diarrhoea.

Infinitely so when I don't have to clean it up.

Though I can still smell it.

Usually, I prefer to get a take-out coffee and go to a local park with it. I'll read, do some puzzles, write some letters. Maybe do a little shopping later.

But the London gloom had turned to London rain, and I didn't much want to go out in that, so I ordered a coffee and took it to one of the tables in the hospital cafeteria.

Primed, as it were with the hint of fountain pen ink.

Obviously, something more workmanlike in black or blue-black, than something more feminine in violet or magenta.

I wasn't consciously looking for Felicia, hadn't thought of her for thirty years at least.

But she was sitting at a table in the middle of a sea of empty tables, so she was easy to notice.

Though it kind of felt as though her past had finally caught up with her, and everyone had heard of her, and shunned her by getting up and leaving the cafeteria as soon as she walked in.

She was of course wearing a hat, though not the kind of close skull cap most commonly seen on cancer patients, but a flamboyantly bright forget me not blue cloche with a rather large brown feather stabbed through the folded-up brim.

And who wouldn't notice a woman alone in a room with a look-at-me hat?

Not that I immediately knew it was her, but that the way her neck curved as she wrote in a notebook seemed familiar.

She glanced up as I looked at her, and held my gaze for a moment before looking back at the book she was writing in.

Dismissing me.

As of no consequence.

I don't suppose she recognised me, I look like what I am now; a short, plump, kindly old lady.

Someone's doting grandmother.

But she looked a bit familiar and it took me a moment to see through the years to the woman I'd once known better than I knew myself.

Yes she'd aged, but she was still thin, still sat as upright as if she had a poker up her arse.

See?

I hadn't even spoken to her and already the bad seed was growing like the unwanted weed it was.

Lord knows why I didn't just leave it alone. Why I had to go and ask was she Felicia Clarke.

Why I had to ask how she'd been and what had happened to her in the meantime.

"Dying," she'd said, "three months max."

I sat down, partly the shock of the news, and partly the shock of the delivery.

It seemed she hadn't grown any more subtle in the intervening period.

"I'm sorry," I said, and I really was.

This wasn't the end I'd wanted for her.

Initially, I'd wanted something short and sharp like a stiletto between the ribs.

But it had been a long time, and I had mellowed and come round to thinking that actually, my life had been incredibly lucky.

Blessed with three children in long term relationships, eight grandchildren and two great-grandchildren!

Amazing to see at Christmas time when the kids take care of all the work and I get to be the best granny ever.

None of which would have happened without her.

I asked, "is there anything I can do?"

And of course, she said no.

"Come to my funeral," she added with a sardonic laugh.

So, I spent my six hours waiting with Felicia, or I suppose, more like she waited with me given she'd just heard the news.

"What will you do?" I asked.

"Go up north to be with my niece," she said, evading my eyes.

I laughed, "nice try, what will you really do?"

She smiled, amused I'd caught her in a lie, "you always could see through me. I've booked into a hospice."

I was fairly sure she'd done no such thing; Felicia wasn't one to wait for anything.

Though maybe she'd booked in, but wasn't planning on arriving.

And if that was the case, she wouldn't be telling anyone in case she left a trail the Police could follow and lay charges.

I didn't press her further.

"Why don't we get out of here, go for cocktails and lunch, reminisce about old times?" she asked.

"I'd like that," I replied.

We went to the Savoy Grill, ate an indecently expensive lunch (which she paid for), and drank so many gin and tonics it seemed like I might be the one throwing up later that night.

"Thank you," she said as she left me, "you've cheered me up no end."

Hugging me, which felt a little final given she'd never been a touchy-feely kind of person.

I watched her weaving in and out of the pedestrians on her way to Charing Cross Tube station, wondering whether I should follow her.

Or warn someone.

Though I had no idea who.

She turned and saw me watching her, grinned her old mischievous grin, waved an outlandishly large wave and disappeared around the corner.

I glanced at my watch and realised I was going to have to get my skates on if I was going to get back to the hospital in time to pick up Danforth.

But at that moment, one of the waiters from the restaurant dashed out and pressed her notebook into my hand, gabbling something and dashing back in.

She was long gone, so I shoved it in my bag and forgot about it, and got back to the hospital just in time.

Poor Danforth was as feeling tired and drained as you might expect. We took a cab to the hotel, and I ordered consommé to the room on the off chance he could keep it down.

The next day we went back North, and life settled down again.

It was only a week or so later I saw her death notice in the newspaper over breakfast.

I exclaimed, and Danforth asked what the matter was.

"That girl I was at secretarial college," I said, "Felicia Clarke. She was discovered dead of cancer in her bed last Tuesday."

"She was a wild one," he replied, "I'm surprised she didn't die sooner."

I grunted non-committally, then mentioned I'd seen her that day at the hospital.

"She's being laid to rest next to her mother in Oxford next week. I think I'd like to go."

His turn to grunt non-committally.

"I always knew," he said.

"Knew what?"

"I always knew I wasn't David's father."

My ears were ringing and I felt dizzy as my blood plummeted to the floor.

He lifted the pot to refill my teacup, spooning in a generous teaspoon of sugar, and nudging the saucer towards me.

"I always knew you didn't love me when I married you, but I thought perhaps I loved you enough for both of us Etta."

I opened and closed my mouth a few times, but really, there was nothing to say about that.

"You've been good to me, so I've never breathed a word to anyone. I just wanted you to know you aren't the only one who can keep a secret."

I don't mind telling you my opinion of him went up a thousand-fold.

"I'm sorry," I said. And I meant it.

"It's all in the past now. You'll be attending my funeral soon enough, and perhaps when you do, your tears won't be crocodile tears."

So I packed my travel handbag again and rediscovered Felicia's notebook on the train, looking for my thermos of tea.

I held it in my hands for a long time, trying to decide whether to open it.

It's not like I was particuarly interested in anything she had to say.

The train shuddered and I dropped it.

Time slowed down as the pages opened and landed written word up.

The thing is that you can't not read things that are written down. You don't form the intention, it just happens.

So before I'd even picked it up I'd read her notes on drugs and side effects, and come to the conclusion it was her suicide plan.

As I said, she wasn't one for waiting.

So I dropped it in the bin when I changed trains at Brimingham.

Felicia's funeral, was surprisingly well attended for a woman who'd been single all her life and only worked for two people.

And a couple of weeks after that, I attended my husband's.

My poor daughter had dropped in on him while I was away and found him slumped over his breakfast table. She'd called an ambulance, but they couldn't revive him.

They thought it would be best not to tell me until I got back given I was away and there was nothing I could do anyway.

I found that I missed Danforth after he was gone. I may not have loved him when I married him, but I grew fond of him over the years, and he will be sadly missed.

Unlike Felicia.

THE END

ABOUT THE AUTHOR

Alexandria Blaelock writes stories, some of them for *Ellery Queen's Mystery Magazine* and *Pulphouse Fiction Magazine.*

She's also written four self-help books applying business techniques to personal matters like getting dressed, cleaning house, and feeding your friends.

She lives in a forest because she enjoys birdsong, the scent of gum leaves and the sun on her face. When not telecommuting to parallel universes from her Melbourne based imagination, she watches K-dramas, talks to animals, and drinks Campari. At the same time.

Discover more at www.alexandriablaelock.com.